For Joey and Ciara ~ two little ones
who are a big part of my world ~ D V B

For little Levi Louis ~ T W

LITTLE TIGER PRESS
An imprint of Magi Publications
1 The Coda Centre, 189 Munster Road, London SW6 6AW
www.littletigerpress.com

First published in Great Britain 2008
This edition published 2011

A CIP catalogue record for this book is available from the British Library

Printed in China • LTP/1800/0270/0711

10 9 8 7 6 5 4 3 2 1

I Love You as BIG as the World

David Van Buren

Tim Warnes

LITTLE TIGER PRESS

London

I love you as **big** as the world.

I love you as

bright

as the sun.

I love you.

And **I know** you love me!

I love you
as blue as the sky.

I love you as long as the days.

I love you as

high as the mountain top.

I love you in so many ways!

I love you as strong

as the wind.

I love you as soft as the dew.

I love you as far as a star.

I love you because . . .

. . . . you are

you!